Welcome to Honeysuckle Hollow

where all the woodland creatures work together
to take care of each other and their environment.

Every animal family has a special job and every day is an
adventure. With their creativity, generosity and sweet
spirit, these friends make chores chockfull of fun.

Meet all the Li'l Woodzeez™ families
in the back of this book.

"There's the Big Dipper!" shouted Pete and Peep

Nighty-Night-Sleep-Tight
Lookout

BY SUSAN CAPPADONIA LOVE
ILLUSTRATED BY CARRIE ANNE BRADSHAW

A Li'l Woodzeez™ Book

*To Chris, David, Steven,
Therese and Mary*

Li'l Woodzeez™ is a Trademark of Battat Incorporated.
Text Copyright © 2017 by Susan Love.
Edited by Joanne Burke Casey.
All rights reserved, including the right of reproduction
in whole or in part in any form.
ISBN: 978-0-9843722-7-0
Printed in China.

"There's the Big Dipper!"
shouted Pete and Peep.

"Where? Where?" asked
their father, Owen.

They pointed up at seven
bright, twinkling stars in the
shape of a soup ladle.

From their watchtower,
the Whooswhoo owls
can see all of
Honeysuckle Hollow.

That's where they run the
Nighty-Night-Sleep-Tight
Safety Service.

If a bike gets a flat tire, they are the first to spot it and they speed to the scene to help. When a snowstorm comes, they spread the good news: "Put on your coat and mittens! It's time to make snowmen!"

"It's time to make snowmen!"

*Clomp-clomp-clomp
clomp-clomp!*

Heavy footsteps came up the
watchtower steps.

"Whoo? Whoo?" asked
Owen. "Whoo's there?"

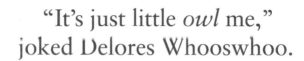

"It's just little *owl* me,"
joked Delores Whooswhoo.

She gave her husband
Owen a kiss on the cheek,
then hugged both
her kids at once.

"How was your day, Mom?" asked Pete.

"Dandy!" said Delores. "First I went to the Bushytails' bakery to investigate the Case of the Missing Pie."

"Blueberry pie?"
asked Peep.
"That makes me hungry.
Can I help you find it?"

"You're always hungry,"
Pete teased.

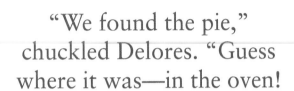

"We found the pie," chuckled Delores. "Guess where it was—in the oven!

"Then I worked on the Case of the School Bell That Won't Ring. I flew to the Bitty Fix-It Shop to see if the mice could repair it."

*Clomp-clomp-clomp
clomp-clomp!*

They heard more footsteps
on the stairs. It was Pete and
Peep's cousin Keith. He was
huffing and puffing.

"Ow!" Keith said, touching his bandaged knee.

"Ow!" Keith said, touching his bandaged knee. "I was walking down the path and slipped on banana peels."

"How? How? How did the peels get there?" asked Owen. "That's dangerous."

While Pete thought
about the mystery, Peep
thought about how good a
sweet banana would taste.

The Whooswhoos flew
to the path to investigate the
Case of the Puzzling Peels.

Owen lit the way with a lantern. The trail of peels went in two directions. They followed it to the dump first.

Pete wrote clues in his detective notebook. Peep took photos of the evidence.

"Aha!" said Delores. "The skunks buried peels around the rosebushes again to help them grow."

"That's a good clue," said Pete. "Now let's follow the trail in the other direction."

Every five or six steps they
found a peel or two. Delores
collected them in her basket.

The trail took them past the
turtles' cleaning service, the
rabbits' farm stand and up
the health center steps.

A sign on the door
solved the mystery:

WE GO BANANAS
FOR GOOD HEALTH

❧

**GET A FREE BANANA SPLIT
WITH EVERY CHECKUP**

"I'll get a checkup!" said Peep.

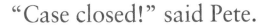

"Case closed!" said Pete.

"Better go! Better go!
I'd better go tell the skunks
their bag has a hole in it,"
said Owen.

"I'll put the peels in the
compost bin," said Delores.

"And I'll get a checkup!"
said Peep.

The Waterwaggle™ Beaver Family
Busy Beaver Launderette

Tapper and Tiny gather the freshly washed laundry off the clotheslines and can't help burying their faces in the crisp bed sheets. Their parents, Lulu and Bobby, put up with their antics, but don't realize how important "sniffing the sheets" will become in Honeysuckle Hollow.

The Handydandy™ Mouse Family
Bitty Fix-It Crew to the Rescue

When something breaks in Honeysuckle Hollow, the woodland creatures skedaddle to the Bitty Fix-It Shop. That's where Mimi and Benjamin, and their kids, Nibbles and Sunny, repair just about anything. From squeaky school desks to broken kites, they're the go-to fix-it mice.

The Bushytail™ Squirrel Family
Tickle-Your-Taste-Buds Bakers

The Tickle-Your-Taste-Buds Bakery makes the most scrumptious pies in town. Maggie and Oliver, along with their kids, Henry and Honeybun, pick and peel apples while Grandma Agnes gets the pie crusts ready. Then it's time to deliver their pies on a bicycle built for two.

The Whooswhoo™ Owl Family
Nighty-Night-Sleep-Tight Safety Service

Delores and Owen, and their kids, Pete and Peep, can see all over town from their watchtower. It's important that everything's in order in Honeysuckle Hollow. One day, after cousin Keith slips on banana peels, they investigate and find a trail of peels that leads to a mystery.

The Whiffpuff™ Skunk Family
Fresh-as-a-Daisy Air Quality Patrol

Thanks to Jasmine and Jacob, and their twin daughters, Iris and Violet, Honeysuckle Hollow smells wonderful. The skunk family picks flowers, berries, herbs and spices, then creates special scents and soaps. Iris and Violet like bathtime, too. Rub-a-dub-dub, two skunks in a tub!

The Tidyshine™ Turtle Family
Clean-as-a-Whistle Tidying Service

Dishes don't stay dirty long in Honeysuckle Hollow. Suds and Sally, and their children, Buster and Bubbles, zip from one kitchen to the next on roller skates. They've earned a spotless reputation for scrubbing pots and pans until every last one is clean.

The Swiftysweeper™ Hedgehog Family
Sweep, Mop, Sparkle & Shine Specialists

When May and Whoosh are too busy cleaning floors, they get their twins, Moppy and Dusty, to help. They're hard workers but cannot resist the opportunity to have some fun. After a mishap that results in a visit to the health center, they realize that life is not all work and no play.

The Hoppingood™ Rabbit Family
Hoppin' Healthy Harvesters

Amelia and Elliot are picking blueberries at their farm When their children, Star and Theo, get hungry, they decide to eat a few of the ripe berries. But one handfu leads to another and soon the whole basket is empty! Will there be enough for everyone in Honeysuckle Hollow now?

The Diggadilly™ Raccoon Family
Reduce, Reuse & Recycle Crew

Debbie and Stripe Diggadilly, and their parents, Rose and Rocco, hate to see anything go to waste. Their business, the Reduce, Reuse & Recycle Crew, specializes in making treasures out of trash and art gems out of junk. All it takes is a little imagination and elbow grease. When Debbie and Stripe find an old fence at the dump, they also find a clever solutio to a problem for their classmates.